Why Corn Is Golden

Acknowledgments

To Carlos Navarrete for the stories "Why Corn Is Golden," "The Chocolate That Turned to Stone," and "Chiapaneco" from the book *Soconusco*.

To the family of Antonio Mediz Bolio for the story "The Sunflower" from the book *La Tierra del faisán y del venado* by Antonio Mediz Bolio.

FIRST PUBLISHED IN GREAT BRITAIN 1984
BY METHUEN CHILDREN'S BOOKS LTD.
11 FETTER LANE, LONDON EC4P 4EE

ENGLISH TRANSLATION COPYRIGHT © 1984 BY ORGANIZACIÓN EDITORIAL NOVARO, S.A.

COPYRIGHT © 1981 BY ORGANIZACIÓN EDITORIAL NOVARO, S.A.

PRINTED IN MEXICO

British Library Cataloguing in Publication Data

Blackmore, Vivien
  Why corn is golden.

  1. Tales, Mexican   2. Indians of Mexico
  —Legends   3. Plants-Folklore
  I. Title   II. Martinez-Ostos, Susana
  III. El maíz tiene color de oro. *English*
  398.2'1'0972 PZ8.1

ISBN 0-416-24810-1

EDITOR: SARAH WISEMAN

DESIGNER: MARCOS KURTYCZ

Why Corn Is Golden
Stories about Plants

Illustrated by
Susana Martínez-Ostos

Text adapted by
Vivien Blackmore

Methuen Children's Books
London

Introduction

Most of the stories in this series come from the days of the old Mexican Indian tribes, before Christianity came to the New World, when people worshipped the elements — rain, sun, wind, and fire. Some come from later times, when the Spanish soldiers brought Christianity to Mexico. They were all tales handed down over the generations, but now only a very few old people in Mexican villages still remember them. For most Mexicans, and certainly for people in other countries, all this myth, folklore, and legend can normally be found only in archives, libraries, and textbooks.

The editor of this series has snatched some of it back and brought it vividly to life in special versions for children everywhere. She has chosen some stories from among those she heard when traveling the countryside talking to people who remembered the old tales; others she selected from the famous anthropological collections. She commissioned brand-new children's adaptations of the stories from Mexican writers and, most important, brought in some of the most talented artists working in Mexico today to illustrate the books in an authentic and vigorous national style.

Welcome to the magic, comical world of folktale where animals, birds, insects, and flowers all speak to you, where nothing is ever quite what it seems, and nothing turns out as you expect.

Contents

Guie'tiiki

Say to the flowers:
the gods summon you to the
Hall of Names and Scents.

When the gods finished making the flowers, they said, "Open your petals on the hills, in the valleys, in the lakes, and on the riverbanks." The flowers heard, and did as the gods had bidden. They opened their petals, they looked beautiful, but they were confused. If anyone said, "Flower," they all turned their heads, thinking they were being spoken to, for they had no names of their own.

The gods said, "We made the animals; this one we called Deer, those we called Rabbit, Tiger, Bear, and Boar. We gave all of them their own special names. We made the birds: Chicken, Quail, Duck, Swan, Mockingbird, Lark, Pigeon, and Dove. We gave all of them their own special names. Now we have made the flowers. Beautiful have we made them, like our soul have we made them; but they do not understand one another, they cannot talk to one another, for they have no names. They know not who they are. This was badly done."

So they called the Parrot and the shining Hummingbird and
said to them, "Fly to the hills and the valleys, to the lakes and
the rivers. Say to the flowers: The gods summon you to the Hall
of Names and Scents."

The Parrot, with its piercing cries, proclaimed the message from the treetops. The Hummingbird with her slender beak whispered the words from flower to flower.

All that day, from dawn to dusk, the flowers filed through the Hall of Names and Scents. The gods spoke; they said, "You are to be called Guie'chaachi; you, Jasmine; you, Gardenia." In this way, they gave them names: Mudubina, Lily, and many, many other names did they give them.

They also gave each one a scent to delight the gods, to delight men and the butterflies. Then on their lips they placed a drop of honey so that the bees would kiss them.

One flower alone did not appear in the Hall of Names and Scents. It did not go for its name, nor for its scent. The sunlight saw it playing with the children, dancing and singing with them. That is why it did not answer the summons of the gods. It preferred the children. It stayed with them and poured its joy out over them.

"It is done. The flowers have all come for their names and for their scents," said the gods. "All except one."

Then they ordered the men and the women: "Do not bring this flower to our altars, for it has no name and no scent, nor any honey on its lips, nor does it have our blessing."

When the children heard the news, they said to the flower, "We love you; you will stay with us; your name will be Guie'tiiki, or Flower Which Stands on Tiptoe."

Every spring, from that day on, when flowers cover the hills, the valleys, the lake, and the riverbanks, the children wait for Guie'tiiki, to pick her up and play with her.

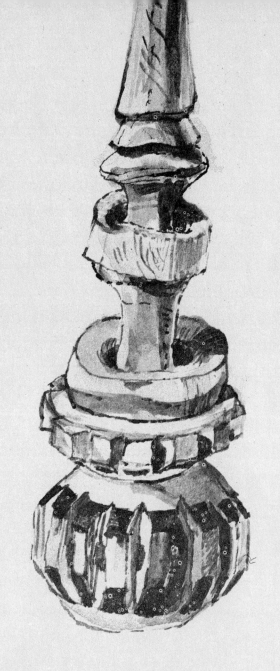

The Chocolate
That Turned to Stone

The village people
started to get tired
and they began to mutter among themselves
and look around
for some way of
getting rid of these rascals.

When the world was still young, there was a tribe of wicked warriors whose only thought was to fight with their neighbors and kill innocent people.

What they liked most was chocolate, so they forced everybody to give them the cocoa beans that were picked. They started by asking for a handful, but little by little they increased the quantity until there was none left for the people in the village. Nobody had the right to a cup of frothing hot chocolate, nor frothing cold chocolate, nor even to a little corn mixed with ground chocolate. The only ones who could guzzle and gulp chocolate until they choked were the wicked warriors, and they got fat and potbellied from doing nothing but sitting and sipping hot cocoa.

The village people started to get tired of this, and they began to mutter and murmur among themselves and look around for some way of getting rid of these rascals.

One day, a little old man went up to the chief of the wicked warriors himself and said, "I have here a little piece of paper with the recipe for some delicious sweets written on it. I've come specially to offer it to you."

"Wonderful!" cried the chief. "Make them for us at once!" So the old man did, and they loved them! There was something strange about these sweets, because the old man took handfuls of cocoa beans to a room where nobody could see them, and came out later with little chocolates that looked like shiny black beans.

He spent the whole of the next day and the next night preparing his mysterious sweets. The following day, all the chiefs, the vice-chiefs, and the underlings were licking their lips thinking of the great pleasure awaiting them. When they couldn't bear to wait any longer, they went to look for the little old man. There was

nobody in the room. All they found was a pile of sweets and the piece of paper with the recipe on it. All that day and all that night, they stuffed themselves with sweets until they couldn't push one more down their throats, and when they saw there were none left, the chief ordered the village people to make more according to the old man's recipe.

They made mountains of sweets for the wicked warriors, and when those greedy ones couldn't eat another sweet they fell into a very, very deep sleep.

When they woke up next day, they found they couldn't get to their feet because their stomachs were all swollen up and felt like lead. They couldn't even walk.

What had happened? The sweets had turned to stone, of course.

The wicked warriors screamed and groaned with the weight of all those stones in their stomachs.

When they found the warriors so defenseless, the people of the village set on them with sticks. They bashed them and mashed

them until they looked like squashed toads. The warriors cried miserably and asked to be forgiven.

The chief himself was caught and flung into the river. Since his stomach weighed so much, he sank straight to the bottom. A few warriors who managed to get to their feet fled in terror and were never seen again. Since then, the village people have been able to enjoy their chocolate in peace. Now they have a right to their hot frothing chocolate, their cold frothing chocolate, and even a little corn mixed with ground chocolate.

The Sunflower

That is why it exists,
to remind you of the light,
which you cannot look
straight at without
being blinded.

This cheerful flower, which is round and yellow like the sun and seems to shine across the fields of Yucatán, grows among the simple flowers and the sweet herbs.

Although it appears to look at you, it is really looking at the sun. You can look at the flower and see a reflection of the sun up above. That is why the sunflower exists, to remind you of the light, which you cannot look straight at without being blinded.

Sit beneath it, and look at it, and think. See how the flower opens to receive the sun's love, the warm clear light that falls onto it. Watch how it bends and turns, little by little, to follow the brilliant sun. Then, when the day sleeps and darkness spreads through the air, the flower closes, as if trying to shut in the light it has received.

Look carefully, and when you find this lovely flower in your path, do not tear it out of the ground, but treat it with love, as you would any other flower or plant. Enjoy it, and appreciate its loveliness, and try to keep some of that beauty inside you.

Why Corn Is Golden

He changed himself
into an eagle
and flew to
the place where the sun rises.

Many years ago when your great-uncles and -aunts and your grandparents were still young, there lived a man who wanted to know all about the Sun.

"Where do you think the Sun lives?" he asked his wife.

"Where can his house be? What door does he come out of? Where does he sleep?"

In those days the Sun was a god and highly respected, and so the wife was afraid: "Don't ask such foolish questions," she answered. "The Sun might get angry and punish you."

However, the man's curiosity was so great that he ignored his wife's words. He turned himself into a sparrow so that he could fly, but the Sun was too far away and the sparrow couldn't reach it, and so the man returned to his house.

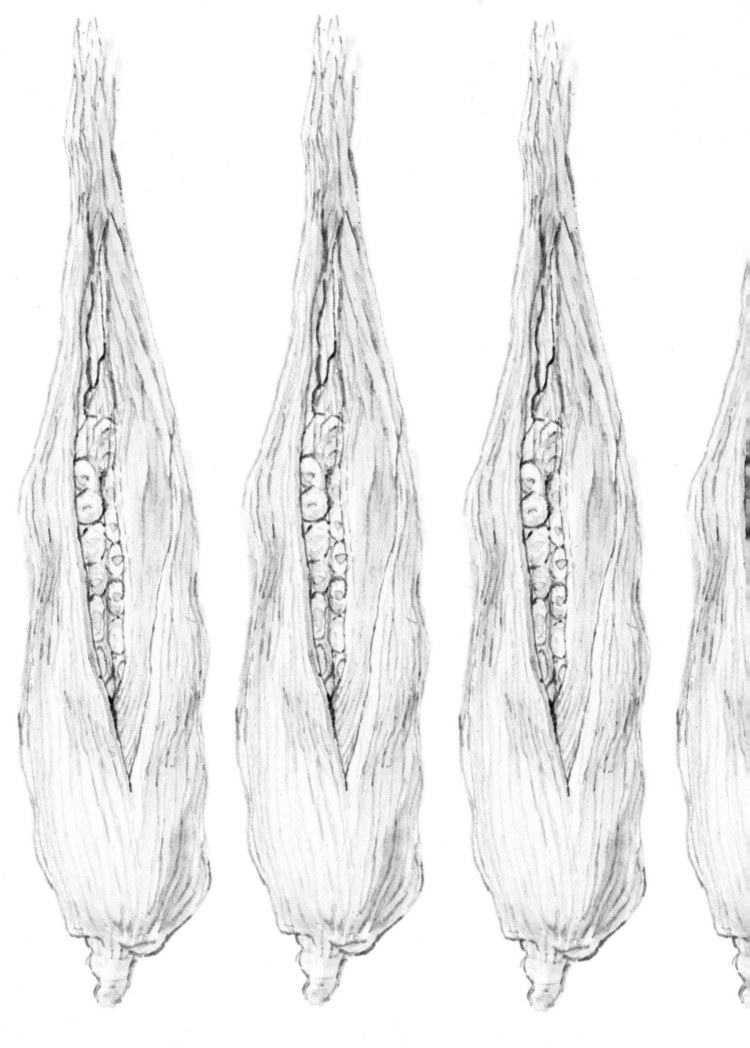

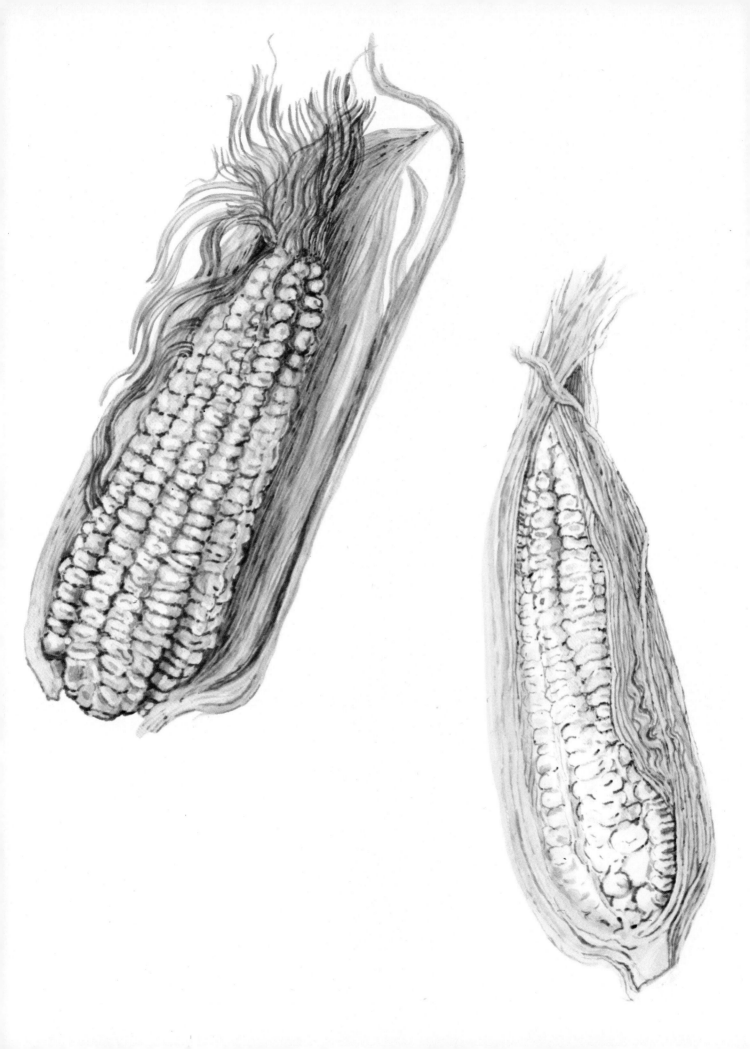

The next day he changed himself into an eagle and flew to the place where the Sun rises, but when he arrived the Sun wasn't there any longer, because he had gone off to warm the young seeds.

"Tomorrow I will wait for the Sun where he sleeps," resolved the man. "I will find the place where he hides." This time he found the end of the earth and the beginning of the sea. He hid behind a tree and watched how the Sun was spilling gold into the water, and how the sea was swallowing it up.

Now the man badly wanted that gold, but gold is heavy and he knew he couldn't lift it by himself. He set off to find someone to help him. After a while he met some dwarves and they said to him:

"Come with us and visit our cave!" And they went together through the door that leads to the center of the earth. The man did not know it, but these little men were really sun rays who warmed the roots of plants and fruit, helping them to grow. They led a good life; they had mice for messengers and ants for friends.

The man entertained the dwarves with stories about the world above. He explained about the gold and asked them if they would like to share it with him. They agreed to this, and they all went together to wait for the Sun, in the place where it sinks into the sea.

They waited on the beach and when at last the great god Sun lowered his golden body into the sea there was so much gold that half of it was swept onto the sand. They picked up all that they could carry and made their way to the man's house.

But the man was not only curious, he was very greedy as well. He really wanted all the gold for himself. When they had gone a little way, he started to cough on the dwarves and they all fell down. Then the man picked up all the gold and put it into an enormous sack and started to run away.

He hadn't got far when he felt the gold getting heavier and heavier — although really it was the man getting smaller and smaller. He shrank to the size of a dog, then a cat, then a bird! His body turned black and feathery, and he grew two big wings. The man's feet curled up and became ugly claws, and now the dwarves saw he was nothing but a buzzard, who looked very ashamed and soon flew away.

The dwarves collected the gold and gave half to the buzzard's wife. She was very happy because she was poor and had many children.

The dwarves carried the rest back to their cave in the center of the earth. They put it carefully into some roots that were growing there. It so happened that these roots were corn roots, and the gold flowed upward. This is the reason why the corn in our land is as golden as the Sun in the sky.

Chiapaneco

Sometimes he appears
as a frail little old man shuffling along,
and at other times
he's blind or lame,
or
he has only one arm.

Nobody knows where Chiapaneco comes from. He arrives in the shape of an old man, a tramp, or a beggar. He does nothing but wander from house to house, asking for a little to eat and a corner to sleep in. He's only allowed to stay because he does no harm and curls up quietly in any corner that he's offered. He eats without chattering and never refuses to help if he's asked to cut corn off the cob, pick a little cacao, or chop some firewood.

But he can't always work, because sometimes he appears as a frail little old man, shuffling along, and at other times he's blind or lame, or he has only one arm.

If people are kind and give Chiapaneco what he asks, their crops grow well and they have enough and to spare. But if they turn him away, their roofs blow off, their walls collapse on top of them, or the plot where they grow their food dries up.

Is someone knocking at your door? You never know — it might be Chiapaneco!

Princess Xóchitl and the Aloe

The next day
they found that the juice,
which had fermented during the night,
had become strong
with alcohol.

One day Princess Xóchitl was walking through a field full of
aloe when she suddenly saw a family of badgers coming out
of a hole they had made under one of the cactuses. They didn't
go far, and soon came back to the aloe licking their chops in
delighted anticipation.

The girl went closer and saw that there was some whitish juice coming out of the hole. She touched it with the tip of one finger and found that it was sweet and good-tasting.

Xóchitl tasted it, brought a clay pot, filled it with this juice, and took it to her father, King Papantzin.

"Father, try this juice," she said.

"It's delicious," he answered; "we'll keep it for tomorrow."

The next day, they found that the juice, which had fermented during the night, had become strong with alcohol. So Papantzin and his daughter cut into the heart of an aloe, making a hole so they could collect the juice of the plant. They called the drink *octli,* and decided to share it with the powerful king Tepancaltzin.

"Daughter, go and show this discovery to Tepancaltzin," said Papantzin.

And so it was that Xóchitl went to offer the *octli* to the king. He was delighted with the drink, but he was even more delighted with the beautiful princess, and soon they were married.

Riddles

I might be an apple
Or I might be a tree
Or I might not be either —
You just try me and see!

If you take off its coat
It will slip down your throat;
If you munch a whole bunch
You won't want any lunch.

I was dry when I set out,
In the garden I grew green.
When the year had turned about
In my house dry was I seen.

One is a pair
With a stone that will grow;
First green it will wear
Then black it will go.

Up in the branches high
There is a small yellow pot;
Never will it be dry
Whether it rains or not.

I've hats stacked on hats —
Nice white hats for rats.
I think I know why
You're starting to cry.

ANSWERS: PINEAPPLE, BANANA, GARLIC, AVOCADO, LEMON, ONION

Susana Martínez-Ostos, who illustrated this book, lives and works in San Ángel in the southern part of Mexico City.